To my sister, Catherine

First published 2003 by Walker Books Ltd
87 Vauxhall Walk, London SE11 5HJ

10 9 8 7 6 5 4 3 2 1

© 2003 Mary Murphy.
Mary Murphy font © 2003 Mary Murphy

The right of Mary Murphy to be identified as author-illustrator
of this work has been asserted by her in accordance with
the Copyright, Designs and Patents Act 1988

Printed in Italy

British Library Cataloguing in Publication Data: a catalogue record
for this book is available from the British Library

ISBN 0-7445-9671-8

Mary Murphy

I Kissed the Baby!

WALKER BOOKS
AND SUBSIDIARIES
LONDON ◆ BOSTON ◆ SYDNEY

'Yes! I fed the baby.
What a hungry
little one!"

"Yes!
I sang to
the baby, and the
baby sang to me."

"I tickled the baby!
Did you tickle
the baby?"

"Yes! I tickled the baby, the wriggly giggly thing!"

"Of course
I kissed
the baby!
I kissed my own
amazing baby ...

...and I'm going to do it again!"

Quackie! Quackie!"

said the baby.